The Escape of Oney Judge

Martha Washington's Slave Finds Freedom

Emily Arnold McCully

Farrar Straus Giroux · New York

Library of Congress Cataloging-in-Publication Data
McCully, Emily Arnold.
    The escape of Oney Judge / Emily Arnold McCully.— 1st ed.
        p.   cm.
    Summary: Young Oney Judge risks everything to escape a life of slavery in
the household of George and Martha Washington and to make her own way
as a free black woman.
    ISBN-13: 978-0-374-32225-0
    ISBN-10: 0-374-32225-2
    [1. Slavery—Fiction.   2. African Americans—Fiction.   3. United States—
History—1783–1865—Juvenile fiction.   4. United States—History—
1783–1865—Fiction.]   I. Title.

PZ7.M478415 Esc 2007
[E]—dc22
                                                                            2005052109

This book is for
Evelyn Gerson's children, Noah and Zelia

*O*ney! Come here, child."

It was Mrs. Washington! Oney ran to her and curtsied, as the house slaves did. Had the mistress caught her doing something wrong?

"Oney, I've had my eye on you," the great lady said. "I see a bright girl who can learn. Tomorrow you will take up a needle and sew alongside your mother in the Mansion."

"Oh, thank you, ma'am," Oney cried. "I'll be glad to work with Mama!"

Oney knew that one reason she had been picked to work in the big house at Mount Vernon was because her father was a white servant and she was light-skinned. But she was bright, too, and loved learning new things. In no time, she mastered the tiny, even stitching Mrs. Washington's sewing circle was famous for.

When the Revolutionary War finally ended, General Washington came home to Virginia safe and sound, a hero. People were calling him the Father of His Country. He was the father of Mount Vernon, too, keeping a stern eye on all the work that had to be done.

The General's valet boasted that his master had brought liberty to the United States. Oney asked him what it meant. "Liberty means the people are free," he said.

"But we're not," Oney said.

"Be careful what you say," he scolded. "You're lucky to be in the Mansion."

Oney knew that. She had seen others working in the fields, and she had seen the terrible welts on a runaway slave's back after he'd been caught and brought back. But for Oney, an even worse punishment than whipping was to be sold to an owner who might work you to death, in a place where you'd never see any of your family again.

Mrs. Washington was raising two grandchildren, a girl, Nelly, and a boy, Wash. Oney was Nelly's playmate when she wasn't sewing. But she was told to leave the room when Nelly's tutor came to teach her lessons.

One day, Mrs. Washington said, "Oney, you've become like another of our children."

Oney bent her head to show thanks. Then she blurted, "Mrs. Washington, please may I learn to read?"

Mrs. Washington laughed. "No, child, you may not. There is no need for you to learn." Oney was crushed, but she hid the hurt.

Instead of lessons, Mrs. Washington gave Oney a new task: she should learn to starch and pleat her mistress's fancy caps. "The General has been elected President of the United States," she said. "We're moving to the new capital up north. You will be my personal maid there."

Exciting as it was, Oney hated to leave her mother and everything she knew behind.

The new President traveled to New York City to be inaugurated. His family followed a few weeks later. Oney managed to keep Mrs. Washington's dresses and caps fresh through dust and heat and cheering mobs at every crossroads, ferry crossing, Revolutionary battleground, speech, and fireworks display.

After a year and a half in New York, the government moved the capital to Philadelphia, in Pennsylvania. Mrs. Washington received elegant lady callers, returned their visits, and shopped for some of the goods the bustling port offered. She fingered gorgeous fabrics from England and France at a dry goods store. Oney studied ladies' gowns to see how they were cut and sewn. Mrs. Washington said that she and the President must not be too fancy, lest they be accused of putting on royal airs in a republic. But her caps became more and more elaborate, and only Oney could fashion them just right.

Nelly liked to sit in the window and watch people walking in the street. Oney sometimes sat with her and marveled at the many black people hurrying by, their heads held high. Where could they be going so proudly? Then Oney was sent to run errands all by herself. The world suddenly seemed new. Without her mistress watching her every move, Oney felt proud, too.

When Mrs. Washington went to visit important ladies, Oney sat with their servants in the back kitchens. She learned that many former slaves had settled in Philadelphia.

Oney tried to imagine being free, but she could not. She worked as hard as a free black, but she wasn't paid. She depended on the Washingtons for food, for warmth, for clothing, for her bed—and they said she was like a child to them.

"How do slaves get free?" she asked one servant.

"Some bought their freedom and moved here. Others ran away or were freed by their masters," she told her. "And there's a law in Pennsylvania that an adult slave who lives here six months must be freed."

Now Oney understood why the Washingtons had started sending some of their slaves back for visits to Mount Vernon.

The President was reelected for a second term in 1792. He and Mrs. Washington would have to live away from their beloved Mount Vernon for four more years.

Oney was in the kitchen in the President's House in Philadelphia one day in the summer of 1793 when a delivery man burst excitedly through the door.

"A ship has come from Haiti loaded with refugees. Toussaint L'Ouverture is leading a revolt of the slaves, and white masters are fleeing for their lives. They call Toussaint the George Washington of Haiti!"

Oney listened with wonder. Like George Washington! But this was black people liberating themselves. "That island is a tiny place," the man went on. "In this big country, we blacks must gain our freedom one by one. The Creator never meant for us to be in chains."

The Creator never meant for us to be in chains. That phrase ran over and over in Oney's mind. It had to be true! She was not a child of the Washingtons; she was one of God's children—just as they were!

But could she ever buy her freedom? Every year on President Washington's birthday she was given a dollar. Last year she used part of it to buy some ribbon to send to her mother. What if she saved the money instead? How many years before she had enough to be free?

She asked Hercules, the Washingtons' cook. He laughed and said, "Some say the master plans to free his slaves when he dies." Then he thought for a moment. "But you belong to Mrs. Washington, and I never heard she had plans to free anyone."

Nelly was begging to go to dancing lessons with her friend Betsy, the daughter of Senator John Langdon from New Hampshire. Mrs. Washington finally agreed to let her go. Oney sewed a new dress for Nelly.

"How beautiful!" Betsy's mother cried. "What fine stitching. Who is your dressmaker?"

"My girl Oney made it," said Mrs. Washington.

"Oh, wouldn't you let me borrow her?" asked Mrs. Langdon. "She could earn a little pocket money."

"Oh dear no," said Mrs. Washington. "I couldn't spare Oney."

Mrs. Washington sometimes allowed Oney to attend the theater with Hercules. They sat with Mr. and Mrs. Jones, who had bought their freedom and now worked with the Quakers, helping runaway slaves to go farther north. The Quakers had even petitioned the government to abolish slavery. Oney had heard the President grumble about the trouble their demands caused him.

One night at bedtime, Mrs. Washington said, "Child, my granddaughter Eliza Custis is getting married. I have decided that after I die you shall go live with her and her husband in Virginia."

Oney stifled a cry. Was she to be owned by Eliza, who treated her badly whenever she came? And owned by Eliza's husband, who could do whatever he liked with her?

Sure enough, a few weeks later, Hercules whispered to her, "That husband of Miss Eliza's sister has already started selling some of her slaves."

If one Custis husband was selling his slaves, so would Miss Eliza's husband. Oney thought she could stand anything but being sold. The Washingtons were about to go back to Mount Vernon for a vacation. Everyone was packing—she could, too, without arousing suspicion. Oney decided she must seize the moment now!

When Mrs. Washington sent her to deliver a message, she went to see the Joneses.
She threw herself on their mercy.

"I must run, now!"

"We will help you," they promised.

The day before the departure for Mount Vernon, Oney packed her bag and took it to the back door, where it was picked up by a boy Mrs. Jones had sent. Oney waited for the Washingtons to sit down to dinner, as they did every day precisely at four o'clock. Then she crept down the back alley and walked quickly toward where the Joneses lived.

While Oney hid there, Mr. Jones searched for a ship's captain willing to take a runaway slave aboard. It didn't matter where the ship was going so long as it carried her far away from the Washingtons. Finally the captain of the *Nancy* consented. After a voyage of five days, Oney landed in Portsmouth, New Hampshire. A free black family took her in, and she told them she would earn her keep by sewing. No one knew her here. Her life was her own!

But one day a few weeks later, as she walked along the main street, a voice called out, "Why, Oney! Whatever are you doing here? And where is Mrs. Washington?"

It was Betsy Langdon, Nelly's friend, home for vacation. Horrified, Oney turned and ran. Betsy would tell the Washingtons she had seen her. Slave catchers would be set on her trail.

Oney stayed indoors doing her sewing and waiting with dread for what might happen next. That turned out to be an unexpected offer of employment from Mr. Joseph Whipple, the customs agent. Oney went to see him, expecting to be asked what skills she possessed. Instead, he began by asking who had given her the idea of running away. Oney was alarmed that he knew who she was. But she answered honestly. "It was my own idea. I would rather die than be given away or sold."

"Didn't the President and his Lady treat you kindly?"

"They did. And I would return to them if they would free me when they die."

"If you go back they will be pleased, and I am sure they would do this for you. There is a boat that departs for the South tomorrow."

Mr. Whipple stood barring the door, waiting for her decision. Oney studied his face. She missed her mother, but she had risked so much for freedom. She couldn't take the chance and let it slip away now. Bowing her head as she had in slavery, she said meekly, "All right. I will go home and pack my things." Mr. Whipple stepped aside, and she hurried from his office.

The family who had taken her in told her she had done the right thing to deceive Mr. Whipple. "The President would have to go to court to force a fugitive slave to return. He won't do that—it would cause a scandal in the North. Stay here and wait him out."

The ship sailed without Oney.

Oney went on working, and as the weeks passed, she tried not to fret about the sword that hung over her new life. She learned to read, making real the dream she had held so long.

Mr. Whipple had not given up. One day he came to Oney and said, "I told the President you would come back if he promised to free you one day. He says he won't bargain with a runaway slave. It wouldn't be fair to the slaves who remained in bondage. I know he would forgive you, but I can't force you to return."

"I must stay here and make my own way," Oney replied quietly.

Months passed, and she met a free black sailor named Jack Staines. They fell in love and married. A year later, Oney had a baby, and Jack Staines went back to sea.

Meanwhile, there was a new President, and the Washingtons had taken up their old lives at Mount Vernon—happy except for the vexation of Oney's escape. Mrs. Washington continued to fume as the months wore on. Why, she kept asking, would a girl treated like a child of the family want to run away from it? When her nephew Burwell Bassett came to dinner and mentioned his forthcoming trip to Portsmouth, Mrs. Washington demanded, "Bring Oney back here with you!"

Oney was reading when Bassett knocked on her door. "Please leave me alone," she said. Bassett tried to fool her. "I can promise you your freedom if you come back."

"I am already free," Oney said.

Bassett argued for a while and finally left. Oney allowed herself a sigh of relief. Perhaps it was really over.

Bassett was staying with the Langdons. At dinner he told another lie—that he had orders to force Oney to board a ship with her baby, who, by law, belonged to the Washingtons, too. John Langdon couldn't believe his ears. Hadn't Oney endured enough? Her baby was legally a slave and could be sold away from her. The senator excused himself from the table and went to the kitchen. There he told a free black he had long employed to go to Oney and warn her to leave town with her baby in all haste!

As soon as Oney heard those words, she wrapped up her baby, raced to a stable, and hired a wagon to take her to a family in another town. Several months later, President Washington died and his wife gave up on ever owning her maid again. For the rest of her long life, Oney Judge had no mistress but herself.

AUTHOR'S NOTE

The story of Ona (Oney) Maria Judge (born c. 1773) has been told many ways. I first read about it in Henry Wiencek's book *An Imperfect God: George Washington, His Slaves, and the Creation of America*, which my friend Elaine Pagels gave to me, hoping that it might contain the germ of a story for me to work with. In his book's source notes, Wiencek credits Evelyn Gerson's master's thesis "A Thirst for Complete Freedom: Why Fugitive Slave Ona Judge Staines Never Returned to Her Master, President George Washington." Gerson summarizes her thesis on the SeacoastNH Web site: *http://www.seacoastnh.com/blackhistory/ona.html*. She was kind enough to read and advise me on my version of Oney's story, as was Mary V. Thompson, Research Specialist, at the Mount Vernon Ladies' Association.

Oney's father was an English indentured servant who left Mount Vernon when his term of four years ended. Her mother and sister remained there, but her brother also went with the Washingtons and their household to the new capital, New York City, to work as a house servant. The Washingtons and their household, including Oney, then moved to Philadelphia, when it became the capital. It was here that Oney first saw free black people and learned of Quakers, who had settled Pennsylvania and were the first group to agitate against slavery.

Martha Custis was a wealthy widow who controlled the lands and slaves of her first husband, including Oney's mother, when she married George Washington. There were many restrictions on what she could do with those slaves, and George Washington was obliged to reimburse her late husband's estate if any escaped. In his book Wiencek speculates that Oney learned Custis heirs were selling slaves in 1796 and she was determined to escape that fate. Hercules, the cook, also escaped soon after Oney's flight to freedom. Washington never took a public stand against slavery, but he did privately hope for its eventual and gradual end and made provisions in his will for the freeing of his own slaves after Martha's death. Oney's sister, Delphy Judge, was freed by Eliza's husband, Thomas Law, on June 26, 1807. We may assume that Oney would have been freed as well. Indeed, Gerson says that Oney never completely escaped the Washingtons—on her death certificate in 1848 she was described as their domestic servant.

Oney lived in proud, independent poverty for the rest of her life, in and around Portsmouth, New Hampshire. Slavery continued to be big business in the North well into the nineteenth century, so her freedom was always precarious. She and Staines had three children. In her old age, strangers often came to visit her, bearing gifts and hoping to hear stories about her life in the President's house. In 1845 an interview with her was published in *The Granite Freeman*. She said she never revealed the name of the ship's captain until after his death, for fear that he'd be punished. This article can be viewed at *http://www.ushistory.org/presidentshouse/slaves/oneyinterview.htm#oney1*.

Senator Langdon was an American patriot, and his warning to Oney was entirely in character. Rufus Wilmot Griswold, an early historian, wrote of him: "He is eminently practical, with sterling good sense . . . there is not one more thoroughly republican in his feelings and tendencies than John Langdon."

SOURCES

Books

Bryan, Helen. *Martha Washington: First Lady of Liberty*. New York: John Wiley & Sons, 2002.

Griswold, Rufus Wilmot. *The Republican Court; or, American Society in the Days of Washington*. New York: D. Appleton and Company, 1855.

Hirschfeld, Fritz. *George Washington and Slavery: A Documentary Portrayal*. Columbia, Mo.: University of Missouri Press, 1997.

Sammons, Mark J., and Valerie Cunningham. *Black Portsmouth: Three Centuries of African-American Heritage*. Durham, N.H.: University of New Hampshire Press/Hanover: Published by University Press of New England, 2004.

Wiencek, Henry. *An Imperfect God: George Washington, His Slaves, and the Creation of America*. New York: Farrar, Straus and Giroux, 2003.

Web Site

http://www.weekslibrary.org/ona_maria_judge.htm